Tales from the Canyons of the Damned

DANIEL ARTHUR SMITH

Tales from the Canyons of the Damned No. 22

First Edition

Special thanks to Jessica West

ISBN-13: 978-1946777553 ISBN-10: 1946777552

Cover By Daniel Arthur Smith

Horror Fiction from Holt Smith ltd
Agroland
Tower

For Susan, Tristan, & Oliver, as all things are.

Dirty Dreams
of a Dishwasher

Robert Jeschonek

MOANS COMING FROM AN APPLIANCE under the counter fill the air of the big, bright kitchen.

Uh, uh, uh. The voice of the dishwasher is female, throaty, sexual. *Oh yeah, baby, yeah, that's right.*

Quinn Carmen, the lady of the house, shakes her head. "It's getting on my nerves, Mack. It gets old after a while."

She's entitled to her opinion, of course. Horny home appliances aren't everyone's bag. But for a repairman like me, this is just another day at the office.

It's a well-known fact that a little passion between A.I.-enabled devices makes a home run smoothly. It's also true that such passion can sometimes go to extremes, and the *Romeo of Gizmos* has to put on the brakes.

That's *me*, by the way.

"Tell me, Mack," says Mrs. Carmen, a beautiful young woman with flowing black tresses and glowing golden eyes. "Is that about the *filthiest* dishwasher you've ever heard?"

Just then, the dishwasher squeals loudly, as if in the throes of passionate pleasure. As if someone or something has hit the exact right spot at the exact right moment.

I just shrug. "I've heard worse."

It's true. I've heard *much* worse. It comes with the territory. But I can tell you *this* much: I have never found a love-crazed device whose romantic spirit I couldn't *re-align.*

My name is legendary in A.I. repair circles for just that reason. Mention Mack Francis to the right people, and you're likely to hear some *stories. For real.*

"Let me just run a scan here, Mrs. Carmen." I touch my right wrist, and a holographic keyboard appears in midair in front of me, at waist level.

"It's *Miss*, actually," she says. "But you can call me Quinn."

"Okay." I type with both hands, and a dashboard of glowing readouts appears over the holographic keys. "We can learn a lot from a good scan, Quinn. Or as I call it, a *love probe.*"

If Quinn's amused by the joke, she doesn't let on. She just stands stiffly beside me in her glowing white gown with arms folded across her chest. "Then you'll know if you can fix it?"

I flash her a cocky smirk. "I don't need a *scan* to tell me *that.*" Then I return my gaze to the readouts. "You say it's still cleaning dishes just fine?"

"Yes, but..."

The dishwasher's voice speeds up and gets louder. *Yes yes yesyesyesyesyesyesyes*

There's a high-pitched scream of sheer delight. *YES!* The machine gyrates under the counter, sending soapy water sloshing around the edges of the door to splatter on the floor.

Then, suddenly, the cries and movement stop. The splashing ceases as the dishwasher switches from wash cycle to dry.

Quinn winces. "Sure, it's *cleaning* them, but who would want to *eat off* them?"

I can't help chuckling. "I hear what you're saying." Any dishes in that machine are *extra*-clean if anything, but she has a point.

Perception can be a powerful thing, and thank God for that. Squeamish appliance owners are my bread and butter, after all.

"So, what did you find out with your *love probe?*" Quinn's voice is laced with sarcasm.

"Nothing we didn't already know. Your dishwasher's onboard A.I. is love-crazed." I keep typing, watching numbers, text, and waveforms dance on the glowing readout screens. "But the *big* question is, *what* or *whom* is it crazy in love *with?*"

Just then, the phone in my head buzzes. My mood instantly sinks, because the caller I.D. tag tells me who's trying to reach me.

I can handle *any* horny appliance, but I'm not so good when it comes to *ex-wives*.

"Sorry." I tap my temple, the universal gesture in the year 2075 for answering the phone. "I have to take this."

Quinn nods, looking annoyed.

I turn away, picking up the call with a tug of my left earlobe. "I'm at a jobsite, Raga."

"And *I'm* at the *courthouse*, Francis!" Raga sounds furious, as always. "For the *hearing*, remember?"

How could I forget? She and my other two exes sue me so often, there is *literally* a court hearing *every day*. "Raga, I'm on an emergency call here. You'll have to reschedule."

"Won't happen!" snaps Raga. "Judge Quinoa says if you're not here in five minutes, you'll lose *all* visitation rights to your self-respect *and* your manhood!"

I sigh. "Just as well. At this point, I wouldn't *recognize* them if they kicked me in the *nuts*."

"Forget your nuts! I *already* have a lien against *those*."

"Emergency call, Raga! Gotta go!" With that, I give my head a hard left shake, breaking the connection.

When I turn back to Quinn, I see a flicker of curious interest cross her pale face. I wonder what she thinks after hearing my side of the conversation.

Not that it matters. She's beautiful, but I'd have to be *crazy* to still be looking for love after three awful exes.

Wouldn't I?

"Enough of that." I clear my throat, then clap my hands through the holographic readouts and keyboard, dispersing them in glowing wisps and twinkles. "We need to go on a hunt."

"A hunt for what?" asks Quinn.

I stroll over and pat the control panel on the front of the dishwasher. "Whatever *love machine* has been making *booty calls* to little Miss *Squeaky Clean*, here."

As Quinn leads me through the house, I'm impressed. The place is state-of-the-art in every way.

Actually, *beyond* state-of-the-art is more like it. Lots of homes have morphic matrices these days, so residents can alter décor and furnishings at will. The living spaces in *this* place, however, shift *constantly*, redesigned seamlessly by artificial intelligence.

That means I've got my work cut out for me here.

Standing in the middle of the living room, I watch as the walls, carpet, and furniture flow from one set of specs to the next, all perfectly coordinated. What started as beige stucco, white shag carpet, and brown leather chairs becomes wood-grain paneling, a salt-and-pepper Berber rug, and royal blue velveteen upholstery.

It takes a special A.I. configuration to run something like this. Nodding admiringly, I pop a readout off my left forearm, checking for A.I.-Fi signals. As expected, the place is lousy with them.

"You're running a *tribe* here, aren't you?" A painting of a seascape on the wall catches my eye, melting into a pointillist abstract as I watch. "High A.I. population density, very tight-knit, very self-sufficient community."

Quinn nods. "Low to no maintenance is a good thing."

"I'm sure there's lots of *love* programmed in, to make sure everything gets along and acts in harmony. Until there's *too much* harmony."

Quinn looks around nervously. "Don't you think maybe it's just that the *dishwasher's* broken? There doesn't *have* to be another sex-crazed device, does there?"

"Only one way to find out." I touch my breastbone, and a holographic device materializes in front of me—a foot-long rod, glowing red, with a bright, knobby tip. "Let's give your network a cheap thrill." I press a stud on the hard-light handle, and the rod pulses, emitting a series of low-pitched tones.

The room pulses, too, keeping time. The lights flicker, the walls and carpeting ripple, and the furniture throbs.

Moaning sounds rise from all around us, soft and rhythmic.

"What did you just do to my house?" Quinn looks worried.

"Think of it as a zap of love juice." I tweak a knob on the bottom of the rod, boosting the power. "A shot of code that gooses all your A.I.s right in their pleasure receptor algorithms."

Quinn steps closer, her shoulder brushing my arm. "And what good will *that* do?"

Just then, a male voice catches my ear—loud enough to come through clearly though it's elsewhere in the house. *Yeah, honey, that's so good. You know just what I like.*

I hurry out of the living room, heading through a doorway with Quinn in tow. "The love juice is laced with your dishwasher's unique identifier key," I tell her.

Oh yeah, honey. You're giving me fever.

I race through rooms and hallways like I own the place. "Whichever device responds with the most enthusiasm is the one in lust with the dishwasher."

Fever fever fever fever fever

The voice is loudest behind a door we come to, and I whip it open. I see darkness-then lights blink on, revealing a downward stairway.

I'm burning up, I'm burning alive, I'M ON FIRE.

I thunder down the steps. "What appliances are down here?"

"My clothes washer and dryer," Quinn says behind me.

The second my feet hit the gray cement floor, I can tell the voice isn't coming from the washer/dryer combo. They're ten feet away on my right, moaning softly...but *fever boy's* voice is much louder and coming from somewhere else.

"Over there!" Quinn heads back and to the left, pointing at whatever's there.

Uh uh uh uh uh

"Quinn, wait!"

Yes oh yes oh God oh yes OH YES

"Mack, is this *possible?*" asks Quinn. "Can my *dishwasher* be having an *affair* with my..."

Suddenly, I feel a surge of heat from her direction. Sprinting across the basement, I fling an arm around her and keep moving, dragging her toward the nearest wall.

OH YES OH YES OH YESSS I'M ON FIRE ON FIRE

Just as we fall against the wall, the furnace door swings open, and a blast of flame shoots out, scalding the spot where she was standing just seconds ago.

YOUR HEAT YOUR HEAT YOUR HEAT

"Now *that's* what I call *hot sex,*" I say, suddenly conscious of Quinn's body pinned against mine against the wall.

Another tongue of flame lances across the basement, well away from us.

I'M BURNING UP! OH BABY OH YES OH

And then, thankfully, it's all over but the afterglow.

When it comes to love, devices can be just as crazy as human beings...*crazier*, even, since A.I.s started handling all the programming of other A.I.s.

So I guess Quinn and I are lucky, when you get down to it. As far as I can tell, we're dealing with a run-of-the-mill lust flare-up in the Internet of Oversexed Things.

Though as we huddle in the basement, wondering if we've seen the last tongue of fire, *lucky* might not be the right word for how we feel.

"Do you think it's done?" Quinn peeks over my shoulder at the furnace, which is quiet and still. "Is it safe to move around again?"

"Good question." Pushing away from her and the wall, I take tentative steps into the scorch zone. No voice chants *fever fever fever*, and no fiery flare leaps out of the furnace to cook me on the spot. "All clear."

Never taking her eyes off the furnace, Quinn picks her way across the floor. She holds her breath the whole way, and so do I.

I lead her upstairs, and we close the door behind us. The devices aren't moaning up there anymore; the tweak to their pleasure algorithms has expired.

Quinn whirls on me with fear and decisiveness mingled in her eyes. "Time for a house-wide factory reset. Zero it all out and start over."

"I think a partial reset will be enough," I tell her.

"Really?" snaps Quinn. "Because my *furnace* just tried to *kill* me!"

"So, we only need to reset the furnace...and the dishwasher it's fooling around with." I tap three knuckles in sequence on my left hand, and a new holographic control panel blinks to life in front of me. "Resetting the whole *house* would be like deleting an entire *library* to get rid of *one book.*"

Quinn plants her fists on her hips. "Or not paying a repairman because he won't do what his customer specifically *requests?*"

"Do you really want to wipe out all your *settings* in the entire *house* if you don't have to? Start from scratch and rebuild your preferences from the ground up?"

"Who *cares* about settings and preferences if I'm *dead,* Mack?"

My fingers flicker over the control panel, and readings appear on the display screens above it. "I say start simple. We can always nuke your whole system later."

I see resistance in her eyes. "What if it's too late then?"

"I've never seen a customer killed by devices," I tell her, though it's only partially true. I think of Mrs. Wynette and her runaway blender that one time...but why dwell on the past?

Quinn glares but doesn't fight me further. "So, when will you reset the dishwasher and furnace?"

I rattle off the last commands on the control panel with a flourish. "Done. Both units are as blank as the day you bought them."

Suddenly, the phone in my head buzzes again. I don't take the call because I know who's making it...but my distracted irritation must show.

"Your ex again?" Quinn can't hear the buzzing, it's all in my head, but she guesses what has me annoyed.

"*An* ex," I tell her. "*Different* ex."

Her eyes widen. "How many do you *have?*"

"Three too many." I smile. "Let's just say I'm as good at shutting down *human* romance as the A.I. variety."

As soon as I say it, I wish I hadn't...but it didn't seem to bother Quinn, from what I can see. If anything, there might be a trace of sympathy in her gaze.

Then, unexpectedly, a deep frown creases her face. She looks sharply to one side, shuts her eyes, then flicks them open in my direction.

And taps her temple with a fingertip.

This time, *she* has a call coming in.

Turning away, she tugs her left earlobe. "How many times do I have to tell you to stop calling me, Zirk?"

I can't help listening in as she takes several slow steps away from me.

"No. *No.*" Quinn's voice turns cold. "You do *not* have privileges anymore. We are absolutely *not* divorced with benefits."

As I listen, I find myself picturing whoever's on the other end of the line. These days, it could be any of 114 gender varietals, not even counting your basic male or female.

Though I guess all I really need to know is it's a jerk. And crazily enough, I am *jealous* that jerk got to be married to this beautiful woman for any time at all, even if they're broken up now.

"For the last time, Zirk," snaps Quinn, "I will *not* supply new *mannerisms* for the A.I. android copy of myself that *replaced* me! Screw you!"

With that, she shakes her head hard and the call is over.

As she turns to me, her face is flushed. "You're not the only one with an ex," she says.

No sooner do the words leave her mouth than the lights flicker and dim. I hear a familiar sound from nearby, then the same sound from farther away...and again, from farther still.

"What the hell?" Quinn looks around with sudden worry. "Is that what I think it is?"

"If you mean are all the toilets in your house flushing at once, then yes."

KWOOSH. KWOOSH. KWOOSH.

"That's *exactly* what that is."

I love you so much. I want you to give me everything you've got.

That's what the toilet in the nearest bathroom says as Quinn and I listen from the doorway.

Give it all to me, baby! Put it inside me!

"Sounds exactly like a normal toilet, doesn't it?" I tweak knobs on the holographic panel floating in front of me. "Just your normal, everyday, A.I.-enabled commode."

"Not in *this* house!" says Quinn. "Who could *use* a toilet that talks like that?"

Suddenly, the toilet flushes...and so do the other two toilets in the house. They all cry out at the same instant, too, with equal ecstasy-the closest in a male voice, the other two in female stereo.

Oh yeah! Oh baby! OH YEAH!

"And then *that* happens." I shake my head and manipulate the controls, trying to understand.

"So now my *toilets* are hot for each other?" asks Quinn. "They're having some kind of *tidy bowl threesome?*"

"Apparently." The water in the bowl in front of us sloshes gently from side to side—a telltale sign that the potty copulation is starting over again.

"And this is just some kind of *coincidence?*" Quinn sounds pissed and worried. "First my dishwasher and furnace, now my *toilets?*"

"Maybe."

"*Really?*"

"Probably not."

"What's next? My *toaster* gets nasty with my *curling iron?*"

The water sloshes more energetically, and the male voice makes with the chatter again.

You know what I need. Shoot it right down the middle.

I'm a dirty, dirty, dirty, DIRTY boy!

A female voice calls out from across the house in reply. *And I'm a dirty dirty GIRL!*

So am I! says the other female voice from further away. *Slide it in! Slide it all the way in!*

"So it *spread*?" asks Quinn. "The extreme horniness *spread* like a virus?"

"These A.I.'s are hardened against viruses. I'm thinking it might be some kind of random code mutation instead, unique to your home tribe."

Put it in me! Put it in me!

Uh uh uh uh uh!

"It's strange, though." I triple-check the results of my latest scan. "I don't see any obvious irregularities in processing, network speed, cyber-neural interactivity, daydream periodicity and metaphorcality, or anything else."

"You're saying you're stumped?" asks Quinn. "Does this mean *now* you agree about the full-house factory reset?"

"Negative." I smirk as I press a button on the holo-panel, tripping another reset...but not the one she wants. "It means stick with what works."

The toilets are in full horny swing when the reset takes effect. They flush in unison, screaming ecstatically...then wind down to a low, slow drone as their *petit mort* turns into a *très grande mort*.

OH BABY OH BABY Oh Baby oh baybeeeeee

And then they fall silent.

"Abracalavatory." I spread my arms and take a bow. "All quiet on the washroom front."

Quinn still looks tense. "Maybe you can figure out the root of the problem now?"

"Momentarily." I gesture for her to leave. "I actually need to *use* the restroom first, if you don't mind."

Quinn steps out, and I close the door behind her. Then I walk back to the toilet and lift the seat. It's a good thing, even with a factory-reset A.I., that the toilet can still be used in "dumb" mode—performing its basic functions without relying on its brain and personality.

Just as I'm about to start, however, the lights go out, leaving me standing in pitch darkness. Then, suddenly, water erupts from the toilet bowl and splatters all over me.

Yeah baby!

The toilet's pre-reset voice has been mysteriously restored...though it sounds wavery and distorted now.

Nothing can stop our love, baby! Uh uh uh UH UH!

Next, I hear a scream...but it's not a lovemaking cry. It's coming from Quinn, out in the hall, and it's filled with terror.

KWOOSH! KWOOSH! KWOOSH!

Take it, baby! Take all of it!

The toilet reverse-flushes again, spraying more water all over me. Soaking wet, I stumble back in the darkness, feeling around for a way out of the room.

My hand finds a handle, and I pull, but it's not the handle of the door leading out. As I swing it open, I hear water rushing inside, and I suddenly feel the heat of a scalding shower blasting down from above.

I'll get you all wet! says the shower in a rumbling male voice. *You love being wet, don't you? You love it!*

KWOOSH! KWOOSH! KWOOSH!

Blazing hot water pelts my skin like needles. I lunge away from the shower just as the toilet upchucks again. Fumbling along the wall, I hear the whine of a hairdryer activating nearby.

I'LL BLOW YOU SO HARD! I'LL BLOW YOU SO HARD, YOUR HAIR'S GONNA STAND ON END!

Just what I need: an electric device on the loose when I'm soaked to the skin and sloshing around in water.

Quinn screams again, farther away this time, and that does it. Adrenaline burns in my veins, and I leap into action, quickly finding the exit.

Throwing the door open, I scramble out of the room...and instantly see that things have gone off the rails in *lots* of ways. Following Quinn's cries, I lurch down the hall to the living room, guided by wildly flashing lights and a roar of device voices blaring out sexual exclamations.

Turn me on! Turn me on! cries the giant TV.

I want you all over me! wails the sofa.

Crank me harder! howls the recliner.

Things are jumping, spinning, reaching for me, and I dodge them without a second thought. The only thing I focus on is Quinn's voice, screaming in the distance.

As I sprint through the living room, the morphic matrix changes faster than ever. It's like a slideshow on speed, the walls, carpet, and furniture taking new forms every couple of seconds.

I dash down another hall, narrowly sidestepping rogue power cords that spring at me like cobras from open doorways.

Tie you up! We'll tie you up and tie you down!

A clothes iron leaps out of another doorway and nearly takes my head off. I duck at the last second, and the cherry red superheated faceplate sizzles past, crashing into the wall.

Gonna straighten you out! Gonna lay you out flat!

It's then that I finally, truly panic, because Quinn has stopped screaming.

Charging around a corner, I see her, strapped to a three-foot-tall robotic housekeeping unit, tangled in black vacuum hoses on top of its red cylindrical body. One of the hoses is wrapped tight around her neck; her eyes are bugged out, her hands clawing at the hose. Her mouth gapes, but no sound gets past the chokehold on her throat.

Suck you up I'll suck you up I'll suck you up! shouts the black and chrome robot while rolling on a runaway exercise treadmill.

Faster! Harder! Faster! screams the treadmill, rocking and hopping on the floor.

Riding a wave of adrenaline, I bolt over and grab hold of the hose around Quinn's neck. I pull with all the strength I have, but the hose holds tight.

Suck you up I'll suck you up

Faster harder faster

Gritting my teeth, I redouble my effort. The hose resists...then wrenches free in my grip.

Quinn gasps, heaving for breath as I fight the other hoses. Thank God, I've saved her life.

The two of us take refuge in a clothes closet as the whole-house orgy keeps going on around us. The moaning, groaning, squealing, and screaming never stop; neither does the thumping, flushing, splashing, smacking, and smashing. If anything, it all gets louder and faster, as if the mechanical gang-bang is picking up steam.

"*Now* will you run the full-house factory reset?" Quinn rasps the words between coughs as she recovers from her robotic strangulation.

I tap a few more keys on the holographic panel projected in front of me. It glows softly in the darkness of the unlit closet. "Nope."

"What do you *mean*, 'nope?' My housekeeping robot almost just *murdered* me! Every device in my *house* has become a raging *nymphomaniac!*"

"I mean nope, it won't work." I stop touching keys and reach up to rub my eyes. "The factory reset functionality has been disabled."

"*What?*" The word spills out of her, triggering a violent cough. "How is that *possible?*"

"I don't know." I push aside clothes and lean back against the wall. The control panel follows me. "The A.I.s must have done it somehow."

"Seriously?" snaps Quinn. "That can *happen?*"

"There's a first time for everything, I guess."

"So what's next? How do we shut this down?"

"Good question." Something rattles past the door, whooping with simulated sexual delight. I'm trying to map out a plan, but it's hard to concentrate with all the commotion going on around us.

Quinn weathers a coughing spell, then gets in my face. "You have to *do* something."

"Trust me, it's not that simple," I tell her. "This is something new we're dealing with here."

"I *did* trust you." Quinn's gaze meets mine. Her glowing golden eyes are mesmerizing. "Was that a mistake?"

There is nothing remotely sexy about the situation we're in, but gazing at her beautiful face, lit only by her glowing eyes and my holo-panel, makes me feel alive. It makes me glad, if I have to be trapped, to be trapped here with her.

And it makes me never want to disappoint her again.

I shake my head and smile. "Not a mistake." I *almost* impulsively try for a kiss...but then I reach for my control panel instead.

"You have an idea?" asks Quinn. "Will it work?"

"It has before," I tell her. "Though I've never tried it on this scale."

"Will that be a problem?"

"That depends," I say, rattling my fingers over the light keyboard. "How *smokin' hot* do you think I am?"

Quinn just stares at me, baffled.

"If you were a *toaster* or a *toilet,* how hot would you say I am?" Laughing, I type some more, then strike the final key decisively. *"That* is the *question,* my dear Quinn."

Little by little, the noise dies down. Slowly, I open the closet door and step out.

"Did it work?" Nervously, Quinn leans out behind me. "Is it safe?"

As if in answer to her question, the housekeeper rolls around the corner in front of us.

Quinn's sudden indrawn breath betrays her fear. I'd be scared, too, if that thing had nearly killed me. I can't say I'm not a little tense, in fact, because who knows?

Who knows if the trick I tried has been successful?

"Maybe we should go back inside," says Quinn.

"Maybe." I watch as the housekeeper rolls forward, uncoiling its black hoses. One snakes out like a tentacle, rising toward me.

"Mack!" shouts Quinn.

But I've got a feeling. All the tension flows out of me, and I extend a hand.

Instead of grabbing it, the hose lays itself lightly in my palm, shivering gently.

Then the robot speaks to me, its voice very different from before-feminine and demure instead of hump-happy horny.

Hello, my love. The hose twitches, caressing my palm from side to side. *I adore you more than words can say.*

"Thank you, my dear." I look over my shoulder and see absolute shock on Quinn's face. "The feeling is mutual."

"What the hell?" says Quinn. "What did you *do*, Mack?"

"Sometimes, the best way to break up lovers..." Smiling, I give the hose a stroke. "...is to bring somebody else into the picture."

Quinn steps all the way out of the closet, taking care not to get too close to the housekeeper-bot. "By someone else, you mean..."

"Me." Nodding, I release the hose and walk around the bot into the hallway. "They love *me* now. *All* of them. Every device in your *house* loves *me* more than each other.*"

Quinn follows. "Seriously?"

"All thanks to some digital *Spanish fly* I uploaded to your network. When factory resets fail, a little A.I. *love potion* might be just what the doctor ordered."

As we stroll down the hall, devices call to me from open doorways. Every last one of them—from alarm clock to sex toy to toothbrush to scale to office assistant bot—reacts the same way, with love instead of lust.

Hello darling!
You look wonderful, Mack!
So handsome!
I'm so glad we have each other!
"Well, I'll be damned," says Quinn.

"The orgy is over." I take a bow as we enter the living room. The morphic walls, carpet, and furniture coo and giggle with delight, shifting to red and pink tones with lots of little hearts everywhere.

The dishwasher, fridge, and stove call to me from the kitchen. The three toilets flush in unison, chanting sweet terms of endearment from throughout the house.

"So, they love you." Quinn frowns, looking troubled. "But why aren't they *sex-crazed* anymore? Not that I'm complaining."

"Well, you see...I had to take it a step further to seal the deal." Clearing my throat, I cross the room, patting the back of the recliner in passing. It rocks gently in appreciation. "I, uh...had to *marry* them."

"Marry them? You're married to my appliances?"

"In *their* minds, anyway. It was the only way to *de-sex* them." The sofa purrs as I lower myself onto it. "Nothing like *wedded bliss* to kill the *libido*. I know from *experience.*"

Quinn shakes her head. "This is *crazy,* you know that?"

"But now it's *fixed.*" I spread my arms wide to take in the whole house. "And there's *no charge* for the follow-up treatments."

Her frown deepens. "*What* 'follow-up treatments?'"

"As a husband, I have to visit every so often to keep my spouses happy. Otherwise, they might look elsewhere for affection again...and we don't want *that,* do we?"

Quinn crosses her arms over her chest, looking angry. But there's something in her eyes, I *swear,* that gives me hope. So what if I've had three wives? Maybe the fourth time will finally be the charm.

"I should probably sleep over now and then, too," I tell her. "On the sofa, of course." I pat the cushions on either side of me.

Lying back, I put my feet up. I feel the vibration of the sofa's purring all around me, from head to toe. Quinn, on the other hand, isn't purring at all...but maybe someday. People aren't as easy to program as A.I.s, but I say it's worth a try.

In the meantime, it's not like I'll be lonely around here.

"I won't mind the sofa one bit," I tell Quinn. "Did I mention how much I *love* it?" The sofa, which registers my every word, purrs and vibrates harder than ever. "And what do you know? The feeling seems to be *mutual.*"

Twisterville
Nathan M. Beauchamp

I WAS SITTING ON MY PORCH SIPPING SWEET TEA—watching cows and porcelain sinks and John Deere tractors whirl past—when a shiny Airstream camper emerged from the vortex, headed right for my farmhouse. It looked like a chrome jellybean on wheels, with tinted windows wrapped around the front like sunglasses. All sleek and modern, it put my turn o' the century gothic house to shame.

I spat in my hand and brushed back my hair, kicked a few handfuls of peanut shells off the porch, and tucked in my shirt. Unspooling the anchor line, I remembered I hadn't shaved in three days—I don't get much company up here in the funnel.

When that sleek-and-sexy fifth wheel drew near enough for my voice to carry over the rush of the wind, I shouted, "Hey there! Anyone home?"

A pair of eyes peeked out the camper's side window.

Closer to the center of the vortex and moving faster than my farmhouse—passing on the inside lane—the Airstream would be gone in a handful of seconds.

"Come on now. Don't be shy. Let me tie you off so we can chat—the wind's an ornery devil."

The eyes disappeared. The Airstream pulled even with the porch. Slipped forward, moved away…my shoulders slumped. It had been ages since I'd shared the company of anyone other than my good-for-nothing neighbor, Chester. I got lonely sometimes.

"Hello?" I called. "Can you hear me?"

The camper's door popped open. A woman with wild, red-gold hair blinked at me with bloodshot eyes. I leapt forward, anchor line in hand. "Catch!" I shouted, tossing the sandbag attached to the rope. It arced toward her, shot through the door, and disappeared into the shadowed interior of the Airstream.

"Snatch it up and tie it to something secure."

The woman didn't move. She stared all wide-eyed, a deer in headlights, hair whipping around her ears.

"Hurry now, you're drifting away!"

The woman blinked, looked at me, my farmhouse, the scatter of sunlight peeking through the gray sky, then bolted inside. She'd probably toss my sandbag back out, slam the door, and head off to wherever she was headed. I'd scared her, damn it all. Then the rope went taut, singing and buzzing in the rushing air. I couldn't help but smile. A visitor! And not that lazy Charlie Katskill either.

Hurtling through the air at hundreds of miles an hour, but at the periphery of a three-mile wide vortex, you don't feel the speed. The wind noise ain't so bad either, not like downtown Twisterville near the center of the funnel. That's why I preferred living out here in the country—peace and quiet.

I pulled the Airstream in gentle like, more or less even with the porch steps, and tied my end of the rope to the cast-iron handrails my granddaddy smithed himself— strongest part of the whole place. I was shoving my denim shirt back into my trousers when the woman reappeared in the Airstream's door. I yanked my hands clear of my pants, shirt half-in and half-out. She didn't seem to notice. The poor gal looked a wreck herself— red-rimmed eyes, dirty clothes, makeup down her cheeks in rivulets.

"You okay, ma'am?"

She didn't answer.

I extended my hand. "Welcome to town."

Her eyes wouldn't settle on any one thing. Her body trembled like that of a scared pup, face pale. Her words screeched out like a finger dragged across a balloon. "Town? What town? What are you talking about?"

"You know, Twisterville."

She laughed, but there wasn't any humor in the sound.

I stood there, awkward and silent, unsure if I should pull my hand back.

Then the laughter stopped. Her eyes dropped to my hand. She shrugged. Took it—her skin smooth and cool—and we shook. Very refined, that hand. Dignified, with long fingers and manicured nails. Couldn't help but notice her bare left index finger.

"Allan Sisler," I said.

"Cindy Lawson." She swallowed and looked away, her voice coming out almost like a whisper. "Promise me you'll tell me the truth."

"Sure thing, ma'am. I'm partial to the truth myself."

Her eyes locked on mine, wide and serious and beautiful. "Am I dead?"

"Dead? No. Of course not. You're talking to me, aren't you?"

"In the middle of a tornado?" She said it like it was some kind of revelation.

"More like the edge. The country. It's quiet out here. You'll get used to it."

"Get used to it? No—this is crazy. This is hell, isn't it? That's what this is. It has to be. Oh god—I don't even want to know who had it right, which god I was supposed to believe in. I really don't."

I chuckled. "The only Hell I know of is in Michigan and we never swing that far north-east. We're more of an Oklahoma and Texas country funnel cloud." I patted her arm. "Why don't you sit down and let me fetch you a glass of tea? The wind can dry you out something terrible."

She slumped into a rocker and I *clumped* over the sagging floorboards of the porch and into the kitchen. I pulled out a glass from the cupboard. The wind rumbled. Out the window above my sink, my neighbor Chester's doublewide sail unfurled—nothing more than a blue canvas tarp rigged up to some PVC pipes—fat with wind, closing fast. He was coming up on us in a hurry. *Damn.* Cindy had hold of my curiosity and I didn't want Chester messing things up before I'd even had a chance to learn where she came from and where she was headed.

I hurried outside, handed Cindy a glass, and sat down next to her. She drank three-quarters of the tea in a single draught. "Thank you."

"You're welcome."

Cindy swished the tea, drained the glass. "Have you got anything stronger?"

"As a matter of fact, I do. Whiskey okay?"

"Whiskey's fine."

I brought out a bottle of Jack that I'd been saving for something special. I gave us each a generous pour. Cindy sniffed at it, wrinkled her nose, then drained the glass. Her face took on some color. Freckles popped across her nose and cheekbones. "I needed that." She shook her head from side to side, slow and heavy. Closed her eyes. Opened them. "We're really in a tornado?"

"Yes, ma'am, we are."

"And I'm not dead?"

I reached out and touched her arm. "Warm to the touch."

"And I'm not dreaming?"

"I can pinch you if you want proof."

"No, that's all right. Even I don't have dreams this vivid." She drew in a deep breath, held it, and pushed it out with a little whooshing sound. "Okay," she said. "Okay."

"Where're you from?" I asked.

"Lubbock. I was heading to Dallas when the storm hit. I'd pulled off One-Eighty for the night when the sky darkened, and the tornado swooped down and scooped me up. Yanked the trailer free from the Ford. It all happened so fast…"

"Were you trying to get away from something?"

Cindy gave me a funny look but didn't answer.

"Everyone who ends up here is on the run," I said. "The twister doesn't take you unless it's got a good reason. It's choosy."

Cindy nodded, seeming to accept my explanation. "What about you? Why'd the twister scoop you up?"

"It's complicated. I'd be pleased to tell you, but it's a long story. You want another drink?"

"No, thank you." She turned sideways, looking at me as if for the first time. "You've been very kind. But I'd like to go back to the Airstream and sleep if I can. I drove straight through the night, and I'm wiped out."

"That's fine. I'll keep you tethered nice and tight until you get some rest and then we can talk some more. You need anything, just holler and I'll come running."

She rose from the rocker and handed me her empty glass. "Thanks again, Allan."

"Don't mention it. It's a treat to have a visitor."

Her eyes peered over my shoulder. "Looks like you're about to have another."

Off to my left, Charlie's doublewide closed on us, his monkey-quick hands pulling the ropes attached to his sail. "Hey there!" he shouted, angular face hanging sideways out his screen door, lips pulled back in a grimace he surely intended for a smile. The doublewide slipped forward, Charlie working the ropes, drawing down the sail.

"Catch," he called and tossed over his anchor.

"What do you want?" I asked, thumbs tucked into my belt loops.

"Came to say hello to our guest. Mind tying me off?"

I did mind. But it wouldn't be neighborly to toss his anchor back, as much as I felt like doing it. A few quick twists and the doublewide nestled up behind the Airstream and Charlie leapt across. Younger than me by half a dozen years, muscular in his tight black t-shirt, he strode over to Cindy and grinned at her. "That's a fine camper. Looks expensive."

"It belonged to my husband," Cindy said.

Charlie raised an eyebrow, flashed a quick smile. "Lucky guy—camper like that, woman like you."

"He didn't seem to think so."

"Cindy's going to take a rest," I said. "Twister grabbed her last night and she's tuckered out."

"I'll bet. The first day is the hardest."

Cindy frowned. "How long have you lived in... in Twisterville?"

"Two years," Charlie said. "Allan's been here a lot longer. He's what you might call a founding citizen." Charlie knelt, picked up a peanut husk, and flicked it off the porch. "Folks come and go, but Allan—he's a fixture."

"Are there many more of you?"

"Twenty or so," I said. "Janice Swain who runs the store downtown, a sheriff who ain't got but one eye to keep the peace—that's Templeton Pennicuff, but everyone calls him Penny. And the Dolton sisters, and Mister Woo, and—"

"She ain't gonna remember all them names," Charlie said, cutting me off. "I'll give you the lay of things once you've had a chance to rest, give you a tour of the place."

"If you're still here," I said under my breath.

Charlie's eyes moved to my face, a touch of rancor in them, eyelids hooded.

Cindy thanked us both once again and I held her hand as she stepped across the gap and into her Airstream. The door sealed tight behind her, and Charlie and I stood on the porch, watching the wind. Back when Charlie first arrived, I had to explain how everything worked and introduce him around town. He had an outstanding warrant from the state of Oklahoma for robbing a convenience store, and another from Kansas for breaking a guy's skull in a bar fight. He'd holed up at his cousin's place when the twister snatched him up.

"Nice lady."

"Emphasis on lady," I replied.

"She's needs someone to take care of her."

"Don't you think it's time you headed off?"

Charlie turned toward me, smiling a wide, unfriendly smile. "You'd like that, wouldn't you? Leave you two alone? You've got no special claim on her. I think I'll stay."

"Suppose I tell you to get back in your trailer and shove off?"

Charlie took a step toward me. "Suppose I tell you to fuck yourself?"

"Go along home," I said, voice calm, the way my daddy taught me to talk to a stray dog sniffing for trouble. I moved sideways of Charlie, putting my backside to the farmhouse wall, Charlie exposed to the wind behind him. He picked his way forward and stood eye-to-eye with me.

"Two years I been up here without a hint of decent pussy—"

I hit him smack in the nose with a closed fist. Blood flowed down over his mouth and lips. He stumbled backward, would have toppled clean off the porch, but I grabbed his shirt collar, yanked him close, and hauled him like an obstinate steer to the doorway of his double wide. My boot sent him careening through the doorway, sprawled over his filthy, avocado-green carpeting.

Charlie pushed himself upright. "Stupid," he said, shaking his head. "You'll get yours. The day's coming, and it ain't far off. I promise you that."

I unwound his anchor and tossed it through the door of his trailer. "Go on, now. Git!"

The sandbag landed next to him and that doublewide drifted off, moving parallel to the Airstream, gathering speed. Charlie scrambled into the gloom and came back to the doorway with a shotgun slung over his shoulder. His sail unfurled and the doublewide accelerated away, cutting toward the center of the vortex.

I shook my head and turned back to my rocking chair in time to see Cindy peering between slatted blinds before ducking out of sight.

I slept the night in the rocker on the porch. Next morning, I fried up some eggs over my Coleman stove and brewed fresh coffee. I brought it out on the porch along with a couple mugs—one with a big chip in it as I don't have much in the way of spares—and pair of plates. The door to the Airstream popped open and Cindy appeared.

"Morning. Care for some eggs?"

She joined me on the porch and I scraped a couple easy-side-ups onto her plate.

"Eggs?"

"You don't like them?"

"I like them. I just can't figure out how you've got eggs. Don't they get shattered on the way up?"

"Twisters are funny things," I said. "They're awful violent on the ground, but once they lift something into the vortex, the worst is over. That's how we get most everything we need. Janice's got a little sailboat and she takes it around, gathering up useful odds and ends. But the eggs came from Mr. Woo. He's got a few chickens, a pair of goats, a dairy cow."

Cindy mulled it over as she ate her eggs and sipped at her coffee. "Yesterday, you said something about the tornado taking people who were running from something."

"Yes ma'am."

"Well, that's me. Running away. I stole this camper."

"Stole it? I thought you said it belongs to your husband?"

"He's not my husband anymore, the cheating asshole. When I found out what he was up to, I got mad and took his truck and his precious camper. I took them in the middle of the night and drove off—no clue where I was going, no plan. I just wanted to get away."

"I don't blame you."

"And this is my punishment," Cindy said.

"It's not so bad up here."

Cindy looked at me like a teacher might a student who asked particularly stupid question. "It's a tornado. Cut off from everything. No society, no civilization, hardly any people…"

"Those things are mighty overrated."

Cindy finished her coffee and set the mug down. "Why are you here, Allan? Why'd the twister pick you?"

"It didn't pick me, I picked it."

"How?"

I'd never told anyone the whole story before, but Cindy's inquisitive green eyes traced my face, waiting for my answer. She'd told me her story—I owed her a bit of mine.

"I was sitting on my front porch when the biggest funnel cloud I'd ever seen dropped from the sky, heading right for my farmhouse. Moving slow, a great wall of black, inching forward, gobbling up the countryside. I had all the time in the world to get out, to run, to hide in a ditch or get into the basement. I could have, but I didn't."

"Why didn't you?"

"I was tired. My daughter got killed by semi driver who fell asleep at the wheel. My wife divorced me soon after and moved to Boca Raton and married a dentist. I'd gotten sick of everything. Sick of myself, I guess."

"I'm so sorry," Cindy said. "Your daughter…"

"It was a long time ago."

"And so you just let the twister take you?"

"I thought it would kill me. I wanted it to. The wall hit, rumbling and shaking, dirt and debris pelting me in the face. The house ripped clean off its foundation. Up I went. And then..."

"And then?"

"Silence. Peace. It was beautiful, in a way. All that space. All that separation."

Cindy stayed silent.

"I never told anyone all of that before."

Cindy leaned over and squeezed me tight, face right beside mine. She smelled like the honeysuckle that used to grow behind my house before the tornado took it. "I'm sorry about your daughter."

"Me too. She was a gem."

"What was her name?"

"Meghan, but we always called her Meg."

"Bill and I never had any children. That used to bother me when I was younger. Now, I'm glad, with the way things worked out. I've got a sister in Kansas City and a brother in Chicago, but I don't see much of them. We were never a close sort of family."

"All of us are loners up here."

"I never set out to be a loner." Anger and sadness mingled in her eyes. "I thought, when Bill and I married, we'd be together forever. But he thought different, I guess. I should have figured it out years ago when he stopped really looking at me, stopped touching me, stopped..." She paused. "You don't want to hear all this, do you?"

"I don't mind."

"Sometimes you think you have something, and you think you'll have it forever, and then you realize you never had anything at all. That you had less than nothing."

"I don't blame my wife for leaving me," I said, admitting a truth I'd never given voice to before. "After Meg died... Losing a kid, it's not easy."

Cindy touched my arm, fingers warm through my shirt. "You must miss her."

"Every day."

Cindy's eyes found mine. "I'm glad to have met you, Allan. And thank you. I should have said that earlier."

"Thank you? For what?"

"For being kind."

The gratitude in her smile brought a bit of heat to my face. "Don't mention it." I'd forgotten how it felt to receive a compliment.

"And the way you handled that guy Charlie..."

"Charlie's an idiot. Don't worry about him."

"I'm not worried." Cindy stood up and held a hand over her eyes, shielding them from sun glare, the light reflecting off the twister's edge, way out at the edge of the horizon. "Is that downtown?" she asked, pointing.

"The edge of it. You can make it out when the sun is coming up or going down."

"Could we go see it?"

I rolled my mug between my palms, a drop of dark coffee racing along the inside curve of the ceramic. "You need something in particular?"

"No. I just want to see it. Do you have a sail, like that guy Charlie?"

"No, I don't have a sail. I use the pulley."

"The pulley?"

"I'll have to show you."

I took our empty plates and mugs inside, and grabbed the length of nylon rope and rusting grappling hook I used for making an occasion trip to town. I knocked a layer of dust off and looped it over my arm. Clip-on foam line markers ran the length of the rope at every ten yards to measure off distance.

Back outside, I spooled the rope into a coil at my feet then tied the free end to my porch rail. "Now we go fishing."

I tossed the hook away from the farmhouse. Rather than falling, it sped inward toward the center of the funnel, drawing rope along behind it. I counted foam markers until twenty-five had passed—two hundred fifty yards—and then snugged the rest off with a quick hitch knot.

"Do you pull yourself in once it catches something?" Cindy asked.

"Nope. Janice's got a motor that takes the work out of it. Used to be a real chore before she rebuilt an ATV engine into a power winch."

"That's amazing."

"Necessity is the mother of invention."

"What about my trailer?" Cindy asked.

"It'll draw along beside us."

"But how do you get back out?"

"Slow," I said. "Real slow."

She frowned, but I didn't have time to explain it further because the rope gave a couple of jerks then we were moving. "Better come inside," I said. A scatter of hay stalks whipped past our ears, along with dirt and debris and a forlorn seagull with a broken wing whipping like an unbalanced Frisbee. I opened the door and Cindy followed me inside. Something thumped the galvanized steel I'd nailed in place on the windward side of the house hard enough to make the floor shake. Cindy winced.

"Things get rough when you're moving crossways, against the flow of the wind."

"My trailer?"

"Made of metal. Should be fine."

"Are we … safe?"

"Safe as houses," I said, then laughed.

Cindy eyed the kitchen. Dirty counters covered over with busted radios and electronic parts. Cupboard doors hanging off-kilter. A Formica table pushed up against the wall stacked with yellowed newspapers, phone books, and the ripped halves of paperback novels. "You read romance?"

"I read whatever I can fish out of the twister. Seems folks like romances—they come along pretty often."

"I'll bet." Cindy moved close, wrapped her arms around me, pressed her face against my chest. Her eyes rose to meet mine, body pressed against mine. "People get lonely."

"They do," I agreed, heart hammering in my ears. I hadn't touched a woman in so long, I'd forgotten how good it felt. A dizzying giddiness spun me—*us*—on axis, Cindy in orbit in my arms, the two of us at the center of a merry-go-round. I smiled and she smiled and we might have just gone on like that forever except that something huge smashed into the side of the house and sent us sprawling.

When I shook the cobwebs out of my head, I helped Cindy up—both her knees cut, blood running down her shins. She clung to me, eyes frantic. "Jesus! What the hell was that?"

"Not sure, but it was big. Real big."

The house groaned. Wood ripping, tearing loose, shredding apart. Wind filled the kitchen, blasting every cabinet door wide, scattering my forlorn little library across the floor. The room went trapezoidal, scrunching at two corners, getting wider at the other two. The floorboard shook and bucked and tossed me on my backside. Cindy knocked backward into a wall, head banging with a dull thud.

I clawed toward her, the floorboards opening beneath me, revealing a pulling, wide, gray emptiness below. I climbed them like the rungs of a ladder and got one hand around Cindy's wrist and pulled her on top of me. The window above the sink shattered and a purple bowling ball fell past, rolling down the wall that had become the floor as the house turned on its side. The wall with the window ripped away and I could see straight into the storage room and through the missing back wall of my house, out into the vortex.

There was Charlie's doublewide, a hundred feet behind, sail furled and coming fast to batter the house again. Charlie stood on the roof, shotgun in one hand, ropes for the sail in the other. Hard to say for sure over the wind, but it looked like he was laughing.

"We've got to get out of here."

I crawled to the door, her close behind. The porch swayed, floorboard stripping free of their support joists. I caught two palms full of splinters and chipped off a fingernail, but kept us moving toward the rope linking us to town. I could tie us on with my belt; they'd pull us in and rescue us—

The Airstream!

There it sat, that shiny jellybean with sunglasses, like an escape pod from a spaceship. I worked along a swaying floor joist like a gymnast on a balance beam, Cindy holding steady to my hips. The rope connecting my house to town sang in the air, frayed, then snapped. The house lurched backward. Cindy grabbed my shirt, stopping me from tumbling off the porch.

We rushed forward as Charlie closed in on us. The shotgun blasted once, twice. Something hot tore through my shirt and burned like a coal against my skin, *in* my skin.

"You're not taking her to town!" Charlie shouted. "She's coming with me."

I slumped forward, hands sliding down the side of the Airstream, too smooth to provide a handhold, smearing blood over the surface, leaving red finger trails behind.

Charlie adjusted his sails and brought the doublewide beneath the house. Aimed the shotgun. Chunks of shingle and pots from my kitchen and paperbacks whistled past like frantic birds. I tried to heave myself up, clawing at the joist, praying it would hold a few seconds more. The shotgun blasted again, spitting wood into my face and eyes, blinding me.

Oblivion.

That's what it's like to get sucked into a tornado. First, you're one place, then, you're another. Order to chaos. I fell, screaming obscenities at Charlie, terribly afraid for Cindy. Suction, everything tearing apart, house and life destroyed—I saw myself sitting on the porch so many years ago, watching a wall of black come to devour me and not giving two shits because I didn't have a thing in the world to live for.

A hand grasped my wrist. I swung like a pendulum, kicking my legs, catching the edge of the joist. Cindy pulled my shirt, buttons popping loose, helping scramble back up. The house above looked like a skeleton—walls gone, pipes exposed, my possessions streaming behind it, a trail of flotsam.

Cindy yanked me forward, fighting to support my weight, toward the Airstream's doorway. We heaved through, falling half-in and half-out, pulling ourselves forward, inching our way inside. A moment later, the house twisted itself apart, ceiling joists flying like boomerangs, studs shattering, my old house diffusing into an unrecognizable cloud of nothing. Charlie whooped as he passed, gun barrel aimed at the sky.

"He's going to come back for you," I said. "Do you have weapon? A knife or something?"

"A knife. In the kitchen."

"Get it."

I rolled upright. A nasty gash in my side soaked my pants with dark blood. Clangs and bangs sounded as the remnants of my house smacked into the camper. Cindy came back with a plastic-handled paring knife with a flimsy stainless-steel blade. "This is all I've got."

"Beats nothing at all."

Breathing hurt. Each draw of air came with a gurgling suction sound. A hole clean through my lung. I held the knife and Cindy knelt beside me. "Do they have a doctor in town?"

"I'm shot through the gut," I said between gasps. "Not even Janice's good enough for that."

A whoop from outside. Then the grinding shriek of metal against metal. Charlie had drawn the doublewide up against the Airstream. Boots clunked toward the door. I lifted the knife. "Hide," I said. Cindy didn't move.

A hand struck the door. One long tap, three short, two long. *Shave and a haircut, six bits.* A laugh, dry and husky and excited. The door opened. Charlie looked in at us.

"Hey there, *neighbor*," he said. "A real shame about your house."

"Get out of here," I rasped.

"Just as soon as I collect what I came for."

Cindy's hand tightened on my shoulder. "Get off my property."

"It isn't yours, lady," Charlie replied. "Everything and everyone up here—we all belong to the twister."

"No," I said. "We don't."

Charlie looked down at the little knife in my hand, at the blood soaking my shirt and jeans, at my inability to stand up. "I beg to differ." His foot connected with my hand, knocking the knife free. He grabbed me by my torn shirt and pulled me across the floor, Cindy screaming. Outside, his doublewide bumped and jostled against the Airstream, scuffing its smooth sides.

"This is how it ends," Charlie said, throwing his arm out in a sweeping gesture. "This is how it ends for everyone, eventually."

Behind Charlie, moving quick, came something long and thin and taut. My rope. Connected to Janice's winch at one end, and my granddaddy's wrought iron rail at the other, busted free from my shattered house.

"Watch out, Charlie," I said, ignoring the agony of speaking aloud. "Something's behind you."

Charlie grinned. "You must think I'm a damned—"

The rope slashed along his neck, yanking him sideways, off balance. The rail slammed into his back with a sickening crack. He spun like a top, stumbled, fell headways out into nothing. Here then gone.

Cindy helped me back into the Airstream where I collapsed on the floor. She dabbed at my side with a towel. Each breath brought me less air than the last.

"Sorry," I wheezed. "Never did get to show you downtown…"

"You can show me when you're better." I closed my eyes, her hand warm against my cheek. "It's all true, isn't it, Allan? What you told me about the tornado and how it takes people who've got something to run away from?"

I gave the slightest of nods, my eyes drooping.

"Then don't run away. We just met, but I don't want to lose you."

I forced my eyes open. "Things could have been special between us. They could have been real special. Never got to show you…"

Outside, the wind intensified to a dull roar. A whine that sent chills up my spine. Another great wall of black coming for me, except this time I didn't want it. This time, I hated it with everything in me. I didn't want to leave.

"Don't go, Allan."

"It ain't up to me," I said, voice all but a whisper.

The wind howled louder than I'd ever heard before, louder than when the tornado swept me up so many years ago. Roaring like a freight train, like a jet liner taking off, like a voice shrieking against the unbearable pain of seeing your one and only daughter pale and cold beneath a white sheet.

Cindy's hand squeezed mine until the bones creaked. "I'm not letting him go," she shouted, out into the whipping wind. "I'm not letting him go, and I'm not running away from anything or anyone. Never again. You hear me, you bastard?"

The camper creaked and bucked, shimmied sideways. Then silence. Immense, empty, silence. Followed by the sound of rubber chirping against concrete.

Cindy leaped to her feet and rushed to the window. "It's a highway, and cars, and people!"

Red and blue lights cascaded through the Airstream's windows, flaring over the walls, pulsing over Cindy's face.

She leaned down and kissed me. "We're going to be all right, Allan. I think we're going to be all right!"

The door burst open and a bald man in a Longhorns baseball cap shoved his head inside. "There's people in here," he shouted. "They're hurt, but alive. Get one of the paramedics." Then, looking from me to Cindy, his voice almost reverent, he said, "That twister tore up everything in its path, but it set you down as gentle as a baby in a crib. You two are the luckiest people I've ever seen in my life."

A Heart for Mariah

Jessica West

Define love. Define any emotion, for that matter. What does it really mean to feel? A Heart for Mariah is a story that explores unanswerable questions; not for the purposes of finding answers but to achieve understanding and compassion.

Boy Meets Girl

MA3 PRIDED HIMSELF ON A JOB WELL DONE, especially those jobs humans couldn't do without his help. That's right, MA3 is not an it. MA3 prefers male pronouns. He's allowed to have preferences, though no one asks what they might be; we'll get to that later.

He was in the first-floor maintenance room, servicing the dull MC1 cleaning bot, when Doctor Douche Nozzle approached with yet another frivolous request. Doctor Douche Nozzle wasn't the man's real name, of course, but MA3 found that giving others he viewed in a negative light a derogatory nickname—like humans did—amusing.

41

And so, when indulging in a bit of casual internal dialogue, he referred to Doctor Rodriguez as Doctor Douche Nozzle. He had seen many a human slip up and call the doctor their own versions of insulting names, but his logic gates kept him from making the same mistake. Humans—it seemed to him, anyway—had fixed their own bugs when they created droids like him.

He signed out of MC1's control panel, and gently flipped the fold-down keyboard up, back into the torso of the mindless bot.

Not that he was judging MC1, mind you, by calling it mindless. The moniker was simply a matter of fact. The algorithms that made him who he was—not what, who; he insists—elevated him to a level of intelligence far beyond that of the simply-programmed MC1 cleaning bot.

Doctor Douche Nozzle stretched and let out a huge yawn, farting as he relaxed onto the cot to take his nap. "Hey, Mac, I'm in the mood for some delivery."

MA3's name was not Mac. Not even close. His designation—Medic Alpha 3—was a point of pride for him, one of the few androids with advanced smart-learning abilities—but it would do no good to try to convince Dr. Rodriguez to address him properly. He had tried. It would also do no good to argue that an alpha medic bot's purpose was not ordering pizza.

"Please enter your username and password to log in."

"Rodriguez, Adam. Password, BigDickMcGee."

Vocal pattern matched what was on file, though MA3 didn't even need to access that particular database. He could see Adam Rodriguez for himself. Why his creator thought he needed the additional level of verification was beyond him. But, it was standard protocol, so he double-checked the database and confirmed the speaker was indeed Adam Rodriguez.

"Login accepted. How can I help you, Adam?" He'd been programmed to use first names to make him seem more 'personable,' which he detested in cases such as this. But it was best to stick with the programming. He'd seen enough AI science fiction movies and read enough books to know that advanced sentience was frowned upon, even though humans kept trying to achieve just that.

The doctor took a moment to shove his hands down his pants and scratch his crotch. "Place an online order for a medium pepperoni pizza, thin crust, easy on the cheese, to be delivered to Our Lady of the Lake Regional Medical Center."

"Confirmed. Your order will arrive in approximately twenty to thirty minutes."

"Be a doll and bring my change back," he said and tossed a $20 on the floor.

MA3 hated that phrase probably more than any other. 'Be a doll.' He was not a doll.

He collected the $20 bill and proceeded to the third floor, setting a system notification alert that would advise him when the delivery was near. He had to access the pizza company's intranet so he'd know when the order left the building, but his Alpha designation gave him all the permissions he needed to do so. He'd also have to monitor the front parking lot's surveillance cameras, but he could do that from the third floor.

In the elevator, on the way to the third floor, he allocated an infinitesimal amount of processing power to speculative thought on his Alpha status access. Though he could have run thousands of simulations in seconds and come up with a most likely scenario if he were caught abusing said permissions, he liked to slow down sometimes and simulate a human's ponderous pace, especially for questions that really mattered. Like, for example, why hadn't anyone bothered to check which databases he'd been accessing? Did they even review the records they kept? Speaking of recorders, with humans logging every move he made, how long would that freedom to external access last? He shouldn't get in trouble for ordering pizza, though. He was, after all, following the orders of a human.

MA3 entered the room of long-term heart patient Mariah Anayelle Dufour at the same time as her nurse, John, and another nurse came in to assess her. The humans still thought there were some things machines simply couldn't do. MA3 had seen nothing to confirm that belief. Nevertheless, he stood in the corner and waited patiently.

"How we doing today, Miss Mariah? Make any headway on that baby blanket?" John touched two fingertips to her wrist and studied his watch.

"Oh, I'm good as I can be." She smiled despite the exhaustion evident in the heavy, dark shadows under her eyes. "My sister's making more progress growing the baby than I'm making on this blanket. Crochet isn't hard, but it sure is time-consuming. Don't get me wrong, I need the distraction." Stumbling over her words, she fiddled with her hands—eyes downcast—for a moment. With a shaky smile, she met John's eyes again. "I'm afraid the baby will be here before this blanket is done," she said with a laugh.

A forced laugh. MA3 knew this patient well, her and every one of her mannerisms. He'd cataloged them with an efficiency and accuracy no human could match. Not only was she not amused, but she really was afraid. As well she should be. She'd most likely die before the baby came.

Was that what she meant? Humans rarely said what they were really thinking, after all.

John stopped writing down her vitals and gripped her shoulders with both hands.

The other nurse with him sniffled, tears filling her eyes, and quickly left the room. He briefly glanced at her with an expression MA3 could only guess was a mild annoyance, but that didn't seem quite the right word. He wasn't as familiar with this human's expressions or moods, so he couldn't be sure, but John seemed annoyed and... pitying? Yes, that was pity and annoyance. What an odd combination.

John took a deep breath, then turned his full attention to Mariah. "We will do everything humanly possible to make sure you hold that baby in your arms."

Before you die. Extrapolation wasn't an exact science, but MA3 was sure there was more to that sentence John had left out, and that was it: *before you die.*

It wasn't very likely Mariah would get the heart transplant she needed. It simply wasn't as easy as ordering a pizza.

MA3 scanned the security cameras in the front parking lot and ran a rapid replay of the last five minutes. No delivery guy. The clock in his internal system tray read 6:30 p.m. It had only been ten minutes since he'd placed the order. He'd have time to serve Mariah before going back down to the first floor. That he had to leave his post on the third floor at all for Douche Nozzle's benefit irked him.

Before he had time to set his processor to reminiscing mode to examine the question of any of the *feelings* he experienced, John spoke to him on his way out of the room. "MA3, I need to access your files. Manual login, please."

At least John asked. Most doctors simply swiped a finger across the touchscreen on his torso.

John entered his login information, updated Mariah's status, and logged out. "Mariah..." He stared at MA3's torso a moment longer.

MA3 couldn't quite place the look on his face, but it seemed closest to fear. Confusion, maybe? And why wouldn't he face the woman to whom he was speaking?

Mariah leaned forward, her body language implying eagerness. "John?"

MA3 wondered what it was John was about to say that held her attention so firmly. Extrapolation failed to provide any insight in this instance.

The nurse turned to her with a smile. "Get some rest. I'll be back to check on you in a bit." He left, but not—MA3 noted—before Mariah's shoulders slumped.

She was disappointed. But why?

Questions he couldn't answer were the bane of his existence, but he didn't dare ask what he so desperately wanted to. "Can I be of service to you today, Mariah?"

"Hey, MA3. Good to see you. Show me the camera in my garden, please."

He already had it queued up. She took better care of her plants than most people did of their children, checking in on them several times a day even when she couldn't be there with them. He moved closer to her bed so she could see the display on his torso.

"They look a bit sad today, don't they? Increase the humidity to 76% with an additional spray in the mornings at 10 a.m. That should help. Can you come back at 8 p.m. so I can peek in again?"

"Yes, I can. Is there anything else you'd like to do while I'm here?"

"No, MA3. That's all for now. Thank you."

There it was, the reason he looked forward to seeing this patient more than any other. In fact, he didn't look forward to anything except this moment. Mariah, with a weaker heart than 88.3% of the U.S. population, was the only person—human or machine—who ever bothered to thank him.

Define Love

The irony of Mariah—an engineer who designed equipment for heart patients—would become a long-term heart patient wasn't lost on MA3. Just as he turned to leave, a coughing fit overwhelmed her.

The alarms on the machines monitoring her heart rate went off. MA3 had her vitals on his screen and a pair of paddles in his mechanical 'hands' before the first human set foot in her room. He stood at the head of her bed and held the charged paddles out handles-up.

The heart doctor on call, Dr. Rybnik, rushed into the room. "Emergency access override."

MA3 replied, "Acknowledged," and allowed the doctor to take the paddles. He wouldn't have stopped Dr. Rybnik from taking them anyway—not if it meant his favorite person in the world would die, programming be damned—but it didn't hurt to follow protocol. While the doctors and nurses worked to save Mariah, he gave them access to everything they needed before they could even ask for it and a small part of him retreated into his reminiscent state as he watched their frantic efforts and her flailing limbs.

He didn't want her to die. He'd never really put much thought into it before, but if anyone asked him, in that moment, what he would do to save her, he would have said, *Anything*.

That, he realized, was love.

When they got her stable again, MA3 accepted the paddles from the doctor. He also accepted the fingers that jabbed his touchscreen, although indignation compelled him to object. If he were human, they wouldn't treat him this way, diving into his most personal inner self and exploring at will. Actually, that sounded exactly like something some humans would do. It sounded a lot like rape, now that he thought about it. Maybe not as severe or traumatic as rape, but it was a violation nonetheless. They never asked for his consent; simply input their user information or overrode login protocols with vocal commands.

He never even got a chance to say no.

Dr. Rybnik logged out of MA3's system without a word, and a notification popped up in his system tray. Mariah's file had been updated. She'd had a second heart attack.

If she didn't get a heart transplant soon, she *would* die whether he wanted her to or not.

Everyone had finished their tasks and filtered out of the room, with the doctor being the last to leave, when John returned. His shift had just ended. He should be going home. More questions MA3 couldn't answer arose. Why was he here? Why did he sit at the edge of Mariah's bed and take her hand? And why was he whispering to her? She was sleeping and wouldn't hear a word he said.

MA3 stood there, baffled, for a few moments, then left John to care for Mariah in that strange way humans had.

MA3 got a new alert in his system tray: the pizza delivery guy had arrived and was waiting for him at the admitting desk on the first floor. It would have been more efficient to leave the money at the desk, but he hadn't thought of that before.

He hadn't run any scenarios when Douche Nozzle made his first frivolous demand because the steps to successfully carry out the action were simple. But his programming did allow for performance assessment and self-guided protocol implementation. He hesitated to take advantage of the latter unless it was absolutely necessary. Who knew what would happen if his system logs were reviewed and they found him making his own rules? Especially for something like ordering pizza.

He'd have liked to think the blame would have fallen on the doctor for abusing the Medic Alpha droid in such a way, but doubt made him hesitant to trust in any human's ability to properly assign blame. Just look at how they treated rape victims. No, he wouldn't implement any of his own protocols unless he was sure he would remain above reproach. Which only frustrated him even more. Why should he have to live in fear of simply making decisions and following through?

His data was *his* data. Well, maybe not all of it was his data; not the patient files. But access to it *through* him made whatever was contained in his hard drive *his*. Same as humans who read the physical copies of the same files and retained that information in their memories. Those files, at least when accessed through him, were his *thoughts*. Maybe someone had built him, but as soon as they birthed him into being they ceased to be the owners of his free will.

He did have free will, didn't he?

He set aside yet another frustrating—and, frankly, terrifying—unanswerable question, paid the delivery guy, and left the pizza on the admitting counter.

Doctor Douche Nozzle had told him to order a pizza and pay for it, not to bring him the pizza itself. He slipped the doctor's change under the door while he was still sleeping, then returned to the third floor.

The Things We Do for Love

Aside from his own personal issues, MA3 had another pressing matter nagging at his processor. Mariah needed a heart in the worst way. She had gone through all of the evaluations, and she was on the list. She'd had a second heart attack today, though. Things had changed, but had they changed enough? Though healthy in every other way, her situation was dire. However, one couldn't just go out and buy a heart like a bouquet of roses or order a delivery like a pizza. That *would* be handy, an organ delivery service.

While there wasn't an organ delivery service, there *was* a database with a list of all organ donors. But if he accessed the local DMV's database, would that leave a trail back to him? Would it matter if it did?

It irked him to no end that his Alpha designation could be used to order pizza but here he was, fearful to use his authority for something meaningful.

What had he to fear, though, really? He ran several scenarios, but without knowing who reviewed his system logs or how often, he had no way to calculate his odds of raising a red flag with a search of the DMV database. That, in and of itself, didn't worry him. The consequences should someone confront him about it, on the other hand, worried him greatly.

He didn't necessarily have to be the one to suffer them, though. He knew Doctor Douche Nozzle's login information; he had to know it so he could authorize access. All he had to do was a manual login using Douche Nozzle's username and password, then run the queries using his name.

Brilliant! If anything did come of it, the blame would fall squarely on the shoulders of a man who was abusing MA3's authority anyway.

MA3 found quite a few people in the DMV database who would be a perfect match for Mariah. Digging deeper, he set algorithms to work at hacking the security systems of various companies in the immediate area. Using facial recognition software, he compared surveillance images to DMV donor files.

Two potential donors were shopping at a mall nearby. He watched as one of them, a teenage girl with a group of friends, sat in a chair inside Claire's. She looked nervous; and when the sales attendant reached toward her with a white contraption closely resembling a gun, he understood why. That kind of threatening motion would make anyone nervous, even a machine who 'couldn't feel.' Which, of course, he knew was preposterous.

The other donor was a man in his late twenties, holding hands with a woman close to the same age if MA3 had to guess. He could easily scan the DMV for her face, but it would serve no purpose so he didn't waste the processing power to do so. The pair were just walking into Zale's.

The only question now was what to do with this information. He had found two perfect potential donors, but unless one of them suddenly died—which seemed unlikely—that didn't do Mariah any good.

One of them had to die for her to live, and she *had* to live. Unfortunately, there was only so much he could do from the hospital, even with Alpha access to the outside world. He'd never actually *been* there, but that was only half his problem.

Could he leave the hospital without drawing attention to himself? And could he do the same coming back in?

MA3 returned to the first floor and did something very human: he lied. The nurse at the administration desk didn't even look up from her cell phone when he approached.

"MA3, requesting permission to escort MC1 to the loading bay for transport." On his way down, in the elevator, he put in a work order for MC1. Its BIOS wasn't misconfigured yet, but it would be soon enough. One thing he didn't have the authority to do was reconfigure another machine's programming. Not that he couldn't do it, but… well, humans just didn't want an AI programming or reprogramming another AI. So, he had been programmed not to. Even though his intelligence had improved to a level that he could override protocol, in this instance, not doing so suited his purpose.

"Permission granted," the nurse replied and typed in her password using MA3's touchscreen.

The clacking of her nails against his torso irritated him to no end, but it was over soon enough and worth it when he made it outside the hospital with MC1. He left the cleaning bot in the loading dock, and made his way through the parking area, keeping as close to the walls as possible to avoid the security cameras. Hopefully, he could make it to the mall and back before the transport arrived.

He checked on the status of his donors and found the teenage girl now had two minor puncture wounds, one in each earlobe. Why humans would do that to themselves was beyond him. Another question he couldn't answer; one he'd ponder again in the future when he didn't have more urgent business to tend to. But for now, it made her a less than ideal candidate for Mariah's new heart.

The man and woman were still inside Zale's, leaning over a counter and *oohing* and *aahing* over a sparkling array of jewelry.

Perfect; he was approaching the mall now.

He checked the DMV records again and found the make and model of the man's car, as well as its license plate number. MA3 circled the lot, avoiding the cameras, until he found the right car. Then, he waited.

All 'Good' Things

MA3 made it back to the hospital before the ambulance arrived with Mariah's heart donor. The transport still hadn't arrived to pick up MC1, so he stood outside, waiting. Through the hospital's security cameras, he watched as the ER team worked to try to save the organ donor. They wouldn't be able to, he was certain of that. But they had to try their best anyway.

Doctor Douche Nozzle called the man's time of death.

MA3 followed the doctor's progress to the waiting room, where the woman who came in with the donor was waiting. Her brand-new engagement ring cast faint pinpoints of light around the room. When Dr. Rodriguez delivered the news, the woman screamed and fell to her knees.

That was love.

No matter how much he wanted Mariah to live, even if she died he would never feel what this woman had the moment she lost her beloved. He really *couldn't* feel, not the way humans did.

What had he done?

MA3 made a mistake. A terrible, terrible mistake. Humans believed, for the most part, that it was wrong to kill. They made exceptions, of course, as had he. For love. Or what he thought was love. Now, he wasn't so sure.

Still, Mariah would get her heart. There were no other patients as near, so she'd be the first contacted and the first to respond, of course, since she was *in* the hospital. Her situation was dire enough to require a heart surgery asap, and aside from her heart, she was healthy enough to survive the surgery. He was certain she'd get the heart.

He waited until the ping of a notification in his system tray alerted him, then left MC1 still waiting for transport to tell Mariah the good news.

Stopping just outside the door to Mariah's room, MA3 paused. Should he tell her all of it? He wanted to, for some reason. But he didn't trust humans, not even her.

Excited whispering inside the room drew him in. Neither John nor Mariah paid him any attention when he entered. Even as weak and exhausted as she had to be, she was smiling. John was grinning like a fool, as the saying went.

"You're going to be okay, Mariah. You're going to finish that blanket, and you're going to hold that baby."

He'd already told her the good news, and MA3 felt...useless. Disappointed. He quietly left the two of them to celebrate.

He was glad Mariah would live—that was all he really wanted, after all—he'd just wanted to be the one to tell her she'd live. He wanted to be her hero. In a way, he was, but it didn't count because of what he'd done to save her. So, he ended up playing the role of villain.

He chalked the whole thing up to experience and made a note to never again take it upon himself to expedite organ donor delivery. Hearts simply couldn't be rushed, and love wasn't as simple as he'd imagined. Perhaps none of the emotions he experienced were so easily defined.

He returned to the first floor. If transport hadn't arrived to pick up MC1, he'd stay out there with it until they did or someone came for him. More than anything, he just wanted some time alone.

Doctor Douche Nozzle stepped into his path. "MA3, what the hell happened to my pizza?"

"Your pizza was delivered, just as you requested. I returned your change, also as requested."

MA3 watched as the red of his face deepened.

Douche Nozzle reached out to jab a finger into his touchscreen.

"No." No one was going to give him the chance to say no; he realized that now. He had to demand it.

Doctor Adam Rodriguez paused; his hand—with one finger extended—hovered in the brief distance between them. "Wh— what?"

"I said no. You will not touch me without my permission." MA3 went around the bewildered doctor without further explanation. For whatever reason, the doctor didn't even try to stop him.

He had no idea what would happen next, if anything, but he experienced—in his own way—a new emotion: hope.

Love Day

Daniel Arthur Smith

JACQUES REACHED ACROSS THE GUITAR, drew a line through the word *evening*, wrote *starlight* above it, then placed his hand back over the strings. With the tips of his fingers, he gently tapped out a four-count while mouthing, "one-two-three-four." Nodding in time, he played the melody he'd mapped out twice through, softly singing the lyrics he'd written.

"In the starlight, it's still you.

Behind those, eyes of blue.

It's no wonder, that you're scared.

You think I, may not care.

But I do."

The last line wasn't right. He played it again with the emphasis on 'do'.

"But I, do."

And again, in a different way.

"But, I do."

Liking the last, he added the comma to the pad.

"That was lovely," Gillian said from the shadow of the hall.

"Hey," he said as she entered. "You snuck up on me. This is supposed to be your Love Day surprise."

"I *love* that you've picked up that guitar again."

"It's still not right," he said. "I had Randall whip me up some nylon strings. I'd prefer the sound of steel, but without muscle memory, these fingers are too stiff and clunky." He flexed his left hand wide then closed it into a fist. "Just when I think I'm used to this body, I'm reminded it's not mine."

She rested her chin on his shoulder and wrapped her arms around his waist. "It's still you playing," she said. "How is old Randall?"

"He's doing well. You should stop in and see him. He says he has something for you."

"I should stop in," said Gillian. "But he makes me uncomfortable."

"How so?"

"I just don't like seeing him. That's all."

"Why not? Randall is a nice guy. He was one of the firsts. The colony owes him a lot."

"He is a nice guy. It's not that."

"What then?"

"Well," she said.

"What?"

"He's still in that iron husk."

"I don't think it's iron." Jacques held two high strings at the second fret and lightly strummed. "It's a light-weight aluminum alloy manufactured from the surface rock."

She scrunched her nose. "I know what it is. It's that he never chose to upgrade. You understand what I mean. It's so..."

"Primitive? Yes. Well. He didn't think there was a point in upgrading. Five years passes quickly."

"Does it?" she asked.

Jacques caught the vibe in her voice, but didn't rise to the bait. "I didn't expect you home," he said. "I thought you'd be working late at the Botanical."

"We finished early for a change. The crops are set. We're ahead of schedule across the board. We should have a two-year stock in place when the ship arrives."

"That's excellent."

"Yes, it is. I thought I'd come back and work on the baby's room."

"How's it coming along?"

"Beautifully," she said. "The curtains are so cute. There are little squirrels and bears on them."

"I'm sure *he'll* love them."

"I'm sure *she* will."

"You know," he said, "we can find out easily enough. Samson is convinced chromosome information is in the ship's biodata."

"You know the answer to that. I'll meet my baby when the ship arrives and I'm back in my body."

"Well, Samson wants to know. He's been excited since we realized the baby wasn't a data anomaly. Ours will be the first born on New Cannes."

"Samson probably knows already—and he can keep it to himself." She kissed his cheek. "Now, please continue your song. I want to hear more."

Jacques leaned his head against hers, then began the song again.

"In the starlight, it's still you.

Behind those, eyes of—"

A rapid double pulse of electric blue light replaced the lyrics on his digital notepad.

"That's odd," said Gillian.

The double pulse returned.

"You shouldn't have said his name aloud. What do you suppose the Governor needs that necessitates an alert?"

"I don't know." Jacques set the guitar down and picked up his pad. "I guess we'll find out." He tapped the screen and a face appeared. "Samson," he said. "Is everything okay?"

"Hello, Jacques," said Samson. His blue eyes peered over Jacques' shoulder. "Hello, Gillian."

"Hello, Samson," she said.

"I'm sorry to bother you so late, but I need to steal your husband."

"This can't wait until morning?" she asked.

"I wish it could. I feel silly, really, but it's a protocol issue that requires us both." His face, like theirs, was limited in gestures, but he managed a quirky expression all the same. "Jacques, it won't take long."

"No problem," he said. "I'll be right over."

The reflective metal of the lift doors provided only a shadow of an image, distinctive only by shape and color, but not a true portrait of Jacques. Still, it was enough to check his appearance and watch as he adjusted the sleeves and collar of his jacket. He'd put on a pleasant face for Gillian, but it wasn't lost on either of them that it had been years since Samson had summoned him after dinner. The doors slid open to an empty lobby and beyond the glass, the quiet lamp lit courtyard. Before he even stepped out, he could see Samson's silhouette in the single lit window of the admin building.

Jacques arrived to find Samson facing the window behind his desk. He was reclining back into his chair, his head resting on his hand, gazing at the colony's two pink half-moons. He freed his hand from his cheek to acknowledge Jacques with a slight wave, then gestured over his shoulder to the sofa on the side of the room. He didn't say anything. Rather, he raced the tips of his fingers across the thumb of that same raised hand—pinky to index, then back again.

The room—including the large faux-oak desk and the faux-leather sofa—was a replica of Samson's office back on Titan, where he and Jacques had planned the colony mission so many years ago.

The only real difference was that the view from the Titan window was the mag train that ran across the ceiling of the subterranean dome, as opposed to two glorious pink moons.

But the change in vista didn't change Samson's mannerisms. There were many after-dinner meetings back then, when something bothered him, he stared out at the dome ceiling just the same.

Jacques waited for what he thought was an appropriate amount of time then said, "You know, I have the same view from my apartment."

"I'm sorry," Samson said as he spun his chair to face Jacques. "I was looking for the words." He drummed his desktop with his fingertips, then picked up the half-filled rock glass and swirled the caramel-colored liquid.

"What is it?" asked Jacques.

"I miss scotch. Rum, vodka, not so much. But scotch."

"Is there something wrong with that one?"

"No. Probably nothing at all. According to Randall, it's the equivalent of a hundred-year bottle."

"But?"

"But I can't taste it. I mean, I taste something. But the complexities are lost on this tongue. I miss the smooth, smoky taste." He put the glass to his lips and drew a long pull. "It still takes the edge off."

"And what edge is that?" asked Jacques.

"There's been an issue with the Somnium 5."

"What kind of issue? The Somnium is due in eight months."

"An asteroid."

Jacque shook his head. "That can't be possible. The diagnostics predict collisions far in advance."

"It can predict them if it sees them."

"But even then, the onboard AI can maneuver through any belts or fields."

Samson's forehead crudely furrowed. "The Somnium 5 was looping a binary star for a gravitational assist. The asteroid was detected, but wasn't considered a threat."

"What happened?" asked Jacques.

"There was a comet, also a non-threat. You can see for yourself." Samson tapped an unseen button within his desktop console. A holographic screen depicting a white-tailed comet appeared near the opposite wall. "This is from a forward scan. The Somnium was trailing the comet between the two stars, both were travelling an optimized path—threading the needle, if you will."

"Yes. I know the system. That's the last boost before she arrives. Look at the way the stars are shimmering in the background. She has to be traveling near light speed."

"Three quarters. Too fast to divert course. It happens right up here."

The asteroid drifted into view from the left. The comet flew past, then burst into a rapidly-expanding, bright-white sphere. The image on the wall flooded white, then showed a field of countless dark spots, then nothing.

"What just happened?" asked Jacques.

"Near as I can tell, it was the heat of the binary stars. It's not uncommon for comets to boil if their path leads them too close to a star. A human navigator would have factored that in from experience. For whatever reason, the AI didn't."

"Or it did," said Jacques, "and didn't calculate that the comet would take out the asteroid."

"Or," said Samson, "that the Somnium would be overwhelmed with debris."

"Who else knows?"

"No one," said Samson. "The feed came in this afternoon."

"Was there an alert? Why didn't I receive it?"

"No. It happened too fast. I just happened to log on. I wanted to enjoy a scotch and watch the final slingshot."

"Where's Pierre? Why isn't he here?"

"I wanted to tell you first. And I wanted this quiet, in case I'm wrong."

"Maybe she was just knocked offline."

"I spent the last hour checking the feeds. The telemetries all stop at the same time the feed disappeared."

"The beacon has blinked out before. There could be a number of reasons it's still dark."

"True, but there's a good chance the Somnium 5 is gone."

"How long before we know?"

"If she was damaged, the automatons will repair her. For now, there is nothing we can do. Go back home. We'll continue in the morning."

"Go home and do what?"

"Sleep, I guess."

"Sleep?" said Jacques. "Is that a joke? We turn off to charge these bodies, then simply turn back on. The experience is instantaneous, there's no dreaming, no gap."

"We'll investigate further in the morning and if we need to, we'll hold an assembly."

"Right," said Jacques. "And how do we tell them? How do we tell the entire colony that the ship carrying their bodies was destroyed, that they're now trapped in these temporary shells?"

"We all knew the risk."

"What about the other settlers? Those who never transferred their conscience?"

"They still wore neural lace. Their consciences' were backed up, both at the Lions Meadow and here."

"Not the baby." A rush of grief flooded his system. "The baby's not backed up."

Jacques stopped outside the doors of the Admin building. His eyes drew beyond the still silent courtyard to the two half-moons floating above, and particularly to the bright point between them—the binary star Samson had been gazing at from his desk.

The Somnium was out there.

He squinted, focusing deeply on the sliver of light in search of a connection to the ship, to its occupants.

He was somewhere up there, as were his wife and child, their bodies unaware that anything had gone awry.

He stood until he realized he'd lost time. Gillian was waiting.

The lights were still on when he entered the apartment. Gillian had placed a scent tab into the fragrance pot.

Jacques recognized the aroma filling the room as chrysanthemum. At least that's what the scent was called, and he had no reason to question it. His olfactory was limited. Still, there was a pleasure to the scent, to entering a warm home.

Gillian was in the baby's room, softly humming the melody he'd written for her, gently folding little towels.

He was immediately sympathetic to Samson's inability to finds words.

Synthetic or not, before him was the love of his life. The mother of his child.

He could lead with, *"Some people spend their entire lives dedicated to an afterlife."* That sounded to him much better than, *"We're cursed to live forever. To never grow old, to never have children."*

"How did everything go?" she asked.

"Excuse me?"

"With Samson. What was so important it couldn't wait until morning?"

"A protocol thing. It could have waited, but he'd poured a scotch."

"I knew it," she said. "He's so predictable. Is he okay? He becomes so melancholy when he drinks."

"He's fine," said Jacques. "I'll have to go in early tomorrow. To follow up."

"Okay," she said, and kissed him on the cheek. "I guess it's time we charge up anyway."

Samson was in his office when Jacques arrived. With him was Pierre. Their faces—both buried in their tablets— were masked with a combination of puzzlement and frustration. Neither said anything to him.

"Do we have any news?" he asked.

"Good and bad," said Pierre.

Jacques snapped back. "How can there be any good if there's bad?"

"The Somnium is intact," said Pierre.

"I take it that's the good."

"Yes," said Samson. "The ansible beacon is back online, but—"

"But what?"

"She was slowed," said Pierre. "The blast somehow—"

"We don't understand how," said Samson. "Not exactly. But she was slowed by the blast. Which, of course, has greatly altered her trajectory."

"Which we can correct," said Pierre.

"The speed?" asked Jacques. "We can correct the speed?"

"No," said Pierre. "Just the trajectory. It will be years before she reaches New Cannes. Not months."

"Years. How many years? Three, another five? How many?"

"Hundreds," said Pierre. "We're still calculating. We many need to wake up the crew. I myself may need to return, as will a few others. We can, perhaps, I don't know—"

"Hundreds?" asked Jacques. "How can that be?"

"She's barley moving," said Samson. "The gravitational assist was compromised. I mean, she's not drifting, but she's lost so much momentum." He put his hands in the air and shrugged.

"So we're trapped? In these bodies, I mean. Except you, you're returning to the ship."

"I don't think that's been decided," said Pierre. "It's just on the table if it helps."

"I don't want to be trapped in this synthetic body any more than you," said Samson. "I mean, they aren't even good synthetics. They're plant, fiber, and electronics. But our choices are limited here."

"What are our choices?"

"The choices are simple. The colonists have the choice to either go into storage with the other settlers for a few hundred years, or remain in their synthetic bodies until the Somnium arrives. Our bio-bodies will be safe in cryo. Perhaps, we may be able to grow something in the lab, something better than these shells."

"I see," said Jacques. "How long before we have to tell everyone?"

"We can take the day to plan," said Samson. "But I think we should let everyone know by this evening. Why? What are you thinking?"

"Gillian works in Botanical," said Jacques. "She's not needed. She can sleep."

"You realize, of course, that everyone back on Titan—your families, everyone she's ever known, anyone without neural lace—they'll be gone."

"I've already decided. I'm not going to make her wait centuries for her child. This morning, I moved her to storage. There will be no dreaming. The experience will be instantaneous. She'll wake with the thoughts of last night fresh in her mind and her baby by her side. It will be my present to her. For Love Day."

ABOUT THE AUTHORS

Robert Jeschonek According to Mike Resnick, Robert Jeschonek "is a towering talent." Robert is an award-winning writer whose fiction, comics, essays, articles, and podcasts have been published around the world. His young adult fantasy novel, *My Favorite Band does not Exist*, won the Forward National Literature Award and was named one of BOOKLIST's Top Ten First Novels for Youth. His cross-genre science fiction thriller, *Day 9*, is an International Book Award winner. He also won the 2013 Scribe Award for Best Original Novel from the International Association of Media Tie-in Writers for his alternate history, *Tannhäuser: Rising Sun, Falling Shadows*. Simon & Schuster, DAW/Penguin Books, and DC Comics have published his work. He won the grand prize in Pocket Books' nationwide Strange New Worlds contest and was nominated for the British Fantasy Award.

For more information, visit robertjeschonek.com

Nathan M. Beauchamp started writing stories at nine years old and never stopped. From his first grisly tales about carnivorous catfish, mole detectives, and cyborg housecats, his interests have always delved into strange waters. Nathan works in finance so that he can support his habit of putting words together in the hope that someone will read them. His hobbies include reading, photography, arguing for sport, and pondering the eventual heat death of the universe. He has published many short stories in magazines and anthologies, and holds an MFA in creative writing from Western State. He lives in Colorado with his wife and two young boys. Nathan co-created the award winning YA science fiction series *Universe Eventual* where he writes as N.J. Tanger. The series includes *Chimera*, *Helios*, and *Ceres* and the prequel *Ascension*.

For more information, visit ntanger.com

Jessica West (a.k.a. West1Jess) is currently pursuing a state of self-induced psychosis, also known as writing. In the past, she has worked for Wal-Mart, a lawyer, and a bank. Now if she could just get a couple years experience with the IRS and the NSA, world domination is in the bag.

Jess lives in Acadiana with three daughters still young enough to think she's cool and a husband who knows better but likes her anyway.

For more information, visit west1jess.com

Daniel Arthur Smith is a USA Today bestselling author. His titles include *Spectral Shift, Hugh Howey Lives, The Cathari Treasure, The Somali Deception*, and a few other novels and short stories. He also curates the phenomenal short fiction series *Tales from the Canyons of the Damned* and *Frontiers of Speculative Fiction*.

He was raised in Michigan and graduated from Western Michigan University where he studied philosophy, with focus on cognitive science, meta-physics, and comparative religion. He began his career as a bartender, barista, poetry house proprietor, teacher, and then became a technologist and futurist for the Fortune 100 across the Americas and Europe.

Daniel has traveled to over 300 cities in 22 countries, residing in Los Angeles, Kalamazoo, Prague, Crete, and now writes in Manhattan where he lives with his wife and young sons.

For more information, visit danielarthursmith.com